THE INTRA-EARTH CHRONICLES

BOOK I: THE TWO SISTERS

THE INTRA-EARTH CHRONICLES

BOOK 1: THE TWO SISTERS

KARA JACOBSON

To John   4-4-22

Always Expect Wondrous Things! :)

atmosphere press

To my lovely, Grandma Kate Nankee.
November 18, 1925 - October 29, 2020

PART 1:
SASHA'S SOJOURN
THE YEAR 2444

- ONE -

This wasn't how it was supposed to go. That's what Adrianne told her before she fell into the ravine; a long, dark, never-ending abyss. Lost to her forever. Sasha had never been one to believe in destiny; that was Adrianne's bit. Adrianne believed that the three of them, strong Jeneva women, could've saved them all, but she knew better. Sasha kept her raven-hair covered and stayed low, which wasn't easy at her towering, 5' 11" height and with a bright red birthmark between her eyes; a devil's mark, former classmates had teased. Sure, you could call Sasha a coward. . .but she was alive.

Sasha traveled through the urban slums by keeping to the shadows. Her stomach rumbled with hunger. The city of Jadeneize, on the banks of the Silver Sea, that was once known as the shining jewel of the East, a thriving center of culture and commerce, was a now a wasteland. All that remained was its charred skeleton.

Those who survived the malfunctioning of the great nuclear machines made a mass exodus out of the city, seeking pockets of shelter on the fringes. She had one mission: to find Enoch.

The birthmark on Sasha's forehead tingled as a

shadow darted behind her. Something rattled, and she dove behind a garbage can.

"Sasha, is that you?" An old man covered in a layer of soot emerged from the shadows, and she crouched lower. "Please," he begged.

Sasha heard footsteps coming closer, and she leapt out of hiding and ran.

"Don't you remember me?" he shouted.

Sasha stopped and glanced behind her, taking in the thin, ragged man with a long, overgrown beard. She shook her head, but something about the man seemed vaguely familiar. Sasha tightened the sheer orange scarf about her head, her last vestige of the old world, and began to turn away. At fifteen years old, Sasha was no stranger to grief or to betrayal. She had reason to be distrustful of men.

"She's alive," he said.

Sasha stopped and stared at the man. "Who?"

"Your little sister. Got your attention, didn't I?" The man cackled and then phlegmatically coughed. Sasha remembered him now, James Ranchert, the custodian of her elementary school. The kids called him "Rag Shirt." That was three years ago, before the world came unraveled.

"You're not well." Sasha turned away from him with tears stinging her eyes.

"Sasha, wait!" James Ranchert tried to catch up to Sasha, but she was already half way up the block. "She's with the people inside!" he yelled.

- Two -

Sasha consulted the address that her mother had hidden within the henna swirls on her palm, and her mind drifted to four days prior. "Find Enoch," Sasha's mother had said. "He will keep you safe." Sasha's mother then tucked Sasha into a hollow depression in the earth beneath the gnarled roots of a large olive tree and charged toward the raiders. That was the last time that she saw her mother.

Sasha wasn't sure what Enoch looked like, but she was sure that she'd know him when she spotted him. And she did. It was an upscale motel that had seen better days—a short dome with a large gaping hole on one side shrouded with vines. The entire motel was covered in moss and creeping ivies, which came back fiercely after the meltdown from spores released to counteract the radioactivity. Sasha opened the arched, heavy front doors and raced up the spiraling staircase to the balcony. She pushed open the parlor doors.

Inside, a tall turbined man with an air of dignity, Enoch, addressed a group of seventeen people, both men and women. They all turned towards her, but she quickly looked away. Enoch motioned to her to join them.

"We must formulate a plan," Enoch said as Sasha sat

down on the floor in front, near two middle-aged women. "Food is dwindling, and the raids are becoming more frequent. People are disappearing; very few children are left in the colony. They are our most precious commodity for building a new world." Enoch smiled at Sasha. "Welcome, dear one."

"What are we going to do?" a woman asked. "We barely have enough food to stave off hunger for ourselves, let alone pay the tariffs to hold back the raiders."

"I can't feed my girl now." A young woman cradled a beautiful babe to her chest.

"Yes, I agree. We can no longer pay the tariffs," Enoch said. "We must make preparations to leave."

"Leave?" an elderly fellow asked. "I have one useless leg. I can't make a bloody journey."

"Rest assured, we will find a way for everyone to safely make the journey," Enoch said. "Pack your things. We leave in two days."

Murmurs resounded among the group as they rose and disappeared behind doors of the dilapidated motel. Enoch approached Sasha. "I had a vision that you were coming."

"You did?" Sasha asked.

"Yes." Enoch gazed at Sasha. "You have a powerful aura; a bright soul. Do not doubt your intuitive abilities, dear one. You are to lead others."

"You have me pegged wrong," Sasha said. "I couldn't even save my sister. The ground opened up. . ." Sasha sniffled and looked away.

"Perhaps, she did not need saving." Enoch placed his hand over Sasha's. "Inside the ravine that your sister fell was not certain death, but a doorway into another world.

One that we will be traveling to together—"

"Wait," Sasha said. "You are saying that my sister, that Adrianne, is alive? No, it can't be. I saw her fall—"

"Please agree to the journey, for it will be marvelous." Enoch's eyes gleamed. "Will you not come?"

Sasha's body ached from grief, and the thought of revisiting the ravine that had claimed her only sister made her shake. Adrianne was gone, and chasing some children's fable of entire civilizations living inside the earth was not going to bring her back. Sasha studied the colorful mosaic reliefs covering the walls of the dome, illuminated from the natural light arcing in from above. Staying behind at the hotel seemed like a much better alternative. She knew how to keep to the shadows.

"There is someone that I would like you to meet," Enoch said, motioning her to follow.

Though bone-weary, she reluctantly obliged and followed Enoch outside. A crimson sunset lit the evening sky.

"Ah, a blessed omen, indeed," Enoch said as he paused, gazing above. "Please," he gestured towards an elderly fellow who happily hummed as he tended to the grape vines. The man was a foot shorter than Sasha with mercurial eyes.

"Shalom, Herald," Enoch greeted the elderly fellow.

"Shalom." Herald nodded, taking in Sasha. "Of whom do I owe the pleasure?" He smiled kindly, his eyes gleaming. "Do I detect an air of nobility?"

Sasha kept her eyes lowered to the ground.

"Your senses are still keen," Enoch stated. "This is Sasha from the House of Jeneva."

"Ah, Sasha. I am honored to have known your mother,

a truly noble and good Madam." Herald reverently bowed.

"Sasha is doubting the existence of the cities within the earth," Enoch interjected.

"Many do," Herald said as he rose with eyes shining. "Let me tell you that they are as real as this world, as real as you or I. My ancestor, who was a brilliant inventor in his time, lived and studied with the beings inside the earth, and the secret knowledge of the entrances below have been safe-guarded by my family for generations." Herald widely grinned. "I know the way," he whispered.

"Herald will be leading our colony to an Intra-earth entrance," Enoch said. "They are expecting us. I do believe that Adrianne arrived a tad ahead of schedule."

Sasha's mind whirled, and though she still doubted, something akin to hope sparked within her soul.

"So, what do you say?" Enoch questioned. "Will you take a leap of faith?"

"It will far exceed your greatest imaginings," Herald said.

"Yes." Sasha couldn't help but smile. "I will go with you."

- σHREE -

They did not have time to pack. That night the raiders attacked. They came in, stealthy as winged predators. The birthmark between Sasha's eyes ached, forcing her awake. Shadows obscured the view of the stars through the large skylight in the dome. Sasha sat up and roused the women sharing the balcony with her. The women rushed to the lower lobby of the motel to awaken their men.

Sasha made for one of many the windows that circled the dome. She leapt outside, climbing down the wall of creeping ivies as the skylight burst apart. She saw them, the raiders, heavily armed and dressed in black with mud plastered to their faces, swarming into the windows through which she had just escaped. Sasha lay flat to the ground, concealed beneath a sprawling grape vine. Gunfire and screams echoed from within the motel. Sasha closed her eyes and covered her ears to the noise; what could she do?

When the motel was long quiet, she climbed back inside. The raiders had shot the men and had taken the women, the children, and the food. Eight men lay scattered across the motel floor. None moved. Herald was gone.

Sasha found Enoch in a corner. She touched his shoulder gently and his eyes opened.

"Ah, dear one. There is still hope." Enoch smiled. "Go to the ravine where you lost your sister. Your guide will be there." Blood pooled beneath Enoch's abdomen. "I am sorry that it is not me," he said as his eyes fluttered. "It will be an amazing journey—"

"No," Sasha said. "My mother said to find you. She trusted only you."

"Have faith," Enoch said, and then in a breath, he was gone.

Sasha covered Enoch with a warm blanket. An old broom stood in the corner. She removed the handle and grabbed a heavy sheet. The raiders hadn't left much in their wake. She remembered one of the women sharing the balcony tucking snacks into a secret niche in the wall.

Sasha climbed the stairs to the empty balcony and slid back the tile in the wall. Inside, were three biscuits and a handful of dried figs. She tucked them into the sheet, securing the sheet to the broom handle with a tight knot. A vessel and satchel hung from her waist. She filled the vessel with water from the Grecian fountain in the center of the lobby and wrapped her orange scarf tightly about her head. In the cloak of night, she exited the motel through the window. She plucked hidden grapes from the underbelly of the vines that had sheltered her from the raiders, adding the plump fruit to her satchel.

Sasha proceeded in the direction of the desert as the dawn birthed a new day. She was going to face the ravine that had claimed her only sister.

- Four -

Once Sasha stepped out of the motel, the desert came on quick. Unless you joined one of the motley gang clans in the city's interior, you were forced to live on the fringes. Enoch's colony had been in a dilapidated motel on the outskirts. The gang clans were gaining territory, sending out emissary raiders to the dwindling colonies. Nowhere was safe.

The city line blurred behind Sasha. Bleak desert surrounded her on all sides, and she had another day's journey to the ravine. Her mouth was parched, and she grew weak from hunger. She needed to rest. A golden eagle called from above. It circled in the sky, and Sasha welcomed its company. Sasha popped a few of the grapes into her mouth, relishing the sweet juices. The eagle continued to call as it flew to the east. Sasha squinted. Up ahead was a cluster of boulders that would make do for a shelter. She tucked away the remainder of the grapes and headed in their direction.

Sasha could not believe her good fortune. In the massive boulder, the wind had carved out a nice crevice large enough for her to crawl into. Something growled from deep inside, and Sasha clasped the broom handle in anticipation. The snarling grew louder until red eyes appeared in the crevice. Two mangy wild dogs lunged at her with teeth bared.

Sasha unleashed the broom handle, smacking the larger one across the face. The stunned dog whimpered and took off, taking its mate with it. Clutching the broom handle, Sasha warily entered the cave. She relaxed when she found it empty. The cave was cool, and Sasha removed the cloth from the broom handle and wrapped it tightly about herself.

Suddenly, a cry came from the back of the cave, and she followed the sound with her eyes. One scraggly pup hunkered in the back, in a niche too small for Sasha to fit. "Come on out, now," Sasha cajoled, but the pup shrank farther back into the cave. She took out a bit of biscuit and set it in front of the hole. As she watched for the pup, sleep overtook her like a thief.

Sasha dreamt of the last time that she saw her sister. A giant crack snaked across the ground, and the earth heaved up. The horses screamed in fear and threw the girls. Adrianne toppled over the edge and clung to the side of the ravine. "I can't hold on!" Adrianne screamed.

Sasha raced to her sister, but it was too late. "Find the machine," Adrianne said. "You have to save them, Sasha! Please. I love you!" Adrianne screamed as she slipped into the abyss.

"Where is she? Where's Adrianne?" their mother shrieked as she arrived at the edge of the precipice. Sasha tearfully shook her head, and she and her mother embraced.

Sasha awoke with a start as something warm stirred beside her. Curled up next to her, was the scraggly pup. It looked to be about five weeks old with wiry, brown fur. Ensnared in a dream, the scraggly pup kicked his legs and howled. Sasha smiled, savoring the pup's warmth.

Sasha finally sat up. The pup opened its eyes and darted to its hole as Sasha chuckled. She scooped up her possessions tucked beneath her; a measly handful of shriveled grapes and figs. Only one biscuit left. She looked toward the pup's hole. He had retreated far inside.

"Good luck, little friend. May your pack soon return for you." She broke off a corner of the biscuit and set it in front of the hole. Sasha cinched the cloth to her broom handle and exited the cave.

The air was crisp and the sun was just beginning its ascent above the horizon. How long had she slept? Twelve hours, or more? Pockets of dew pooled around the rock and she drank. She pulled a canteen from her waist and filled it as best she could. Sasha sighed. She doubted that half a canteen of water would be enough to get her through the desert.

"The Great One will provide." Adrianne's voice echoed in her head. I sure hope so, baby sis. Sasha touched her heart in gratitude that the Great One had indeed provided shelter last night. Was her sister still alive? And living inside the ravine? Sasha held onto the hope, no matter how farfetched, as she proceeded in the direction of the rising sun.

- Five -

The sun beat down as Sasha wove along the sandy ridge of dunes. Mirages formed in the distance. She sipped the last few drops from her canteen. How foolish she was to think that she could make the journey in two days, and alone.

Sasha wiped away a tear. Up until a week ago she had had both her mother and younger sister. Together the three had survived, slinking in and out of different gang clans, gathering what knowledge they could before moving on. But then, Adrianne tragically fell, and when they returned home from their futile quest, raiders had dismantled the clan. Her mother fought back.

Sasha slid down the side of the large dune to the bottom. She needed shelter, to wait out the sun's blaring rays. She untied the heavy sheet from the broom handle and stuck the handle into the side of the dune. She draped the sheet over the handle, creating a small tent shelter. She crawled in, and as the sand cooled around her, she drifted off to sleep.

It was the same dream. Sasha raced to her sister who clung to the side of the ravine, but it was too late. "Find the machine," Adrianne said. "You have to save them,

Sasha! Please. I love you!" Adrianne screamed as she slipped into the abyss.

Sasha watched her sister fade into blackness. But this time, there was more. Adrianne landed softly on something white and buoyant. Adrianne stood facing a curious, lush green world, and was approached by concerned beings speaking a familiar, yet incoherent tongue. . . "Welcome to Mu's Outpost."

Sasha shivered, rousing herself from sleep. She had lost time yet again! She slid the sheet aside and bright stars dotted the sky. Something howled in the distance. Sasha wrapped the sheet to the end of the broom handle, popped the last of the pitiful grapes into her mouth and resumed the journey.

She stopped and listened. The world was silent. A darkness blew across the sky, blotting out the stars, and the desert sand danced around her feet. Sasha tightened the sheer orange scarf about her head. She glanced behind her and she saw eyes, catching the light, bounding towards her. With nowhere to run, Sasha turned and faced the eyes with her broom handle poised and ready in her hand.

The wind picked up and the sand blasted against her skin. The creature yipped as the wind pushed it back. Sasha recognized the scraggly pup. She leapt forward and snatched it up by the loose scruff of its neck. The pup yelped but quit fighting as she safely tucked it into her satchel. She pushed on. She would need to find shelter soon or risk being erased by the sands.

- Six -

Sasha dreamt. Adrianne smiled and the sisters locked arms; Sasha was twelve, and Adrianne eight. The girls and their mother wore bright silk party gowns with sheer jeweled shawls. It was a time when life was perfect; before the great nuclear machines that powered the cities malfunctioned. Sasha was all dressed and ready to go. She waited for her sister in the alcove beside the window.

Sasha savored the familiar view from her family's flat: sunlight refracted off of the sides of the great domes, casting arcs of rainbow light throughout the valley, sky shuttles zipped through the air and hundreds of stories below was the tram, the silent light rail train that glided along the lush, manicured gardens.

"Adrianne, did you feed your felines?" the girls' mother called, rousing Sasha from the window.

The family's two large, languid Siamese cats wove in and out between Adrianne's legs as the girls got ready for the party.

"They aren't just mine," Adrianne said as she put down her hair brush and lifted one of the sleek cats into her arms, "but, of course." The cat loudly purred.

"They favor you," the girls' mother said as she peered

into the girls' room. "Put him down," their mother ordered. "He could claw a hole in your gown."

Adrianne groaned as she set the cat down onto her bed and gave him a good pet before joining her mother and Sasha in the kitchen. The girls kissed their father on the cheek and followed their mother to the teleport capsule in the back of the apartment. Their mother punched in the codes to their destination and they were instantly transported to a solstice party, in honor of the old ways.

Friends welcomed the sisters and their mother, placing lays of flowers around their heads and handing them flasks of bubbly punch. Suddenly, a great roar was felt as much as heard. The sirens blared. "Take shelter! Take shelter at once," echoed over the intercom. The large dome shook and swayed.

Sasha awoke to a yelp beneath her. She removed the heavy sheet that covered them. The sandstorm had passed and evening in the desert was upon her. The pup struggled to climb out of the satchel. She rolled to the side to free the pup and rolled into a horse's forelegs. The horse danced nervously and Sasha scurried to her feet, clasping the pup to her chest. A nomad peered down at her from atop a massive black steed. Sasha was about to flee, when the nomad removed their turban. It was a woman.

The woman motioned for Sasha to climb onto the horse's back. The horse snorted uneasily at the pup. "Shh, shh," the nomadic woman said as she patted the horse. The steed calmed, and Sasha, who collapsed from dehydration and hunger, allowed herself to be lifted onto the horse's back.

Sasha's head bounced up and down as the horse galloped. They rode over miles of dune until dawn. Sasha opened her eyes just as they arrived at a settlement on the banks of a blue and green oasis. Lush vegetation sprouted up on the banks of the turquoise water. Vibrant red, orange, purple, and yellow blooms blossomed from within the green moss and creeping ivies. Modern structures remained intact and the sweeping gardens flourished. Here it was as if the meltdown had never occurred. Other nomads came out to greet them. They removed their turbans; they were all women. A woman with kind violet eyes helped Sasha off of the horse.

"Welcome, dear one. I am Katra, and these are my kin. We live in a void space invisible to the outside world. We perform daily meditations to raise the vibration of the space, of this oasis, to cloak it from the outside world. We are very much present, but outsiders do not perceive us. They move on by."

The pup whimpered.

"Ah, we have another guest," Katra said. "You must both be very hungry. Tonight, we will have a feast in honor of your arrival."

- $\mathcal{S}$EVEN -

A group of eight women clothed in loose, colorful shawls whirled in a ring in orchestrated dance. A fire burned behind them where food was being prepared. Sasha sat next to Katra with the pup in her lap. The pup lifted its nose to the air and whined for food.

"Soon, little one," Katra said as Sasha gazed at the dancers. "Marvelous, are they not?"

"Beautiful," Sasha said. "Thank you for finding me in the desert and bringing me here. I fear that I would not have survived."

"The Great Spirit said that I would be delivered an adept," Katra said. "But I did not fathom that it would be so soon. Spirit is mysterious, is it not?"

Sasha shifted uncomfortably and pulled the pup in close.

"Do not fear." Katra smiled. "It is bound to be a grand adventure." The dancers whirled towards them, bowed, and then took their seats. "Ah, the food is ready. Vegetarian, but it really is quite delicious. You will see."

The women hummed and touched their hearts as they sat cross-legged in a ring. A large bowl of hummus and rice dripping with a savory bean sauce was set down in the center of the circle. A bowl of pita bread was passed around which they exuberantly dipped into the rice and hummus, grinning with pleasure. Plates of dried figs, juicy mangoes, papayas and decadent cakes were in abundance. The Great One had once again provided, and Sasha and the pup feasted hungrily with grateful hearts.

- EIGHT -

In the desert oasis, Sasha and the pup slept in a first-level guest flat within a tall structure with a domed apex. The pup lay curled at Sasha's feet snoring lightly. A warm breeze blew the sheer window curtain open and closed. Sasha stepped out. The village was quiet. Bright stars dotted the clear night sky. The moon reflected off of the serene waters. Sasha raised her hands in the air and then touched her heart. How fortunate to have ended up in this oasis with Katra and her kin. Sasha went back inside the flat and slept soundly beside the pup.

She awoke to a peculiar sound. There it was again. A gong? Sasha raced out of her guest flat with the pup bounding after her. Sasha stopped quickly, and the pup bounced off of her leg. She lifted the scraggly pup to her chest and watched. In the brilliant morning light, the women were standing in a circle on the edge of the village with arms raised. A ripple of energy rose like a wall, shrouding the oasis.

A war party astride horses sounded a gong. The leader, a Caucasian man with steel-colored eyes and robed like a prince, with a massive gun strapped to his chest, absently gazed into the village. Sasha shivered as something about him struck her as familiar. The soldier's horses snorted uneasily, but the war party continued past.

When the soldiers disappeared from sight, Katra approached Sasha. "We are seeing soldiers more frequently," Katra said. "Unfortunately, they are traveling in the same direction that we will be going. Are you well rested?"

"Yes, thank you," Sasha said. "I feel better than I have been in a long time."

"Excellent, we will set out tomorrow, at sun rise," Katra said. "Today, enjoy yourself and the rejuvenation offered by the turquoise waters."

Katra entered her dwelling and returned with swim wear and a towel. Katra handed them to Sasha, "the oasis waters truly are healing. Enjoy."

Sasha disappeared inside the guest flat and reappeared in the swim suit, a pastel blue, thigh length wispy shirt and bottoms. She wrapped the towel around herself and wove her way down to the water. Women that she passed on the way smiled and nodded.

Sasha walked into the blissfully cool water. She dove and swam far out to the center. Her mind drifted to frolicking in the water with Adrianne. She splashed Adrianne, and her little sister giggled and splashed back. Then, the vision changed.

It was the day that the machines malfunctioned. She, Adrianne, and her mother escaped the dome with their friends at the party before it toppled, but their family dome had already collapsed.

The council dome still stood. They raced inside in search of their father. Just as they entered, they heard gunfire and ducked behind the massive stone column in the center that supported the structure. Armed men filed out, but not their father. When it was quiet, their mother signaled for the girls to move. A man with a large gun strapped over his chest, scavenging for supplies, spotted them. The girls tried to run, but he grabbed them. They screamed. The girls' father emerged and lunged at the man. The armed man shot their father and then ran off.

The girls and their mother raced to their father lying on the council floor.

"I am so sorry, Trish," he said. Their father reached out and locked arms with Adrianne and Sasha. "Girls, I love you so much. . .you are my life, my joy."

"Hold still, now," the girls' mother, Trish, said. "You are going to be alright." Trish ripped a bit of fabric from the hem of her party dress and applied it to his belly wound.

"Go 20 kilometers to the east through the desert to an up-dwelling of earth, the Eastern Blue Ridge Mountains. There is a hill shaped like a Hallows Eve witch's pointy hat. Inside is a cave with a backup machine. . .enough to power a new city. . ." their father's voice drifted off.

"Wait, no, Tanner!" Trish cried. "Stay with us! We need you."

"I love you so much." Tears glistened in his eyes, and then, he was gone.

The girls lay for a long time beside their father and wept.

The vision changed. Adrianne, Sasha, and Trish raced to the Eastern Blue Ridge Mountains on horseback to find the witch's hat-shaped hill with a cave where the backup machine was stored. But the malfunctioning of the great nuclear machines had disrupted the earth's tectonic plates, and the earth rumbled and shifted below their feet. A giant crack snaked along the ground, and the earth heaved up. The horses screamed in fear and threw the girls. Adrianne toppled over the edge and clung to the side of the ravine. "I can't hold on!" Adrianne screamed.

Sasha raced to her sister, but it was too late. "Find the machine," Adrianne said. "You have to save them, Sasha! Please. I love you!" Adrianne screamed as she slipped into the abyss.

But when Sasha and her mother located the witch's hat-shaped hill and entered the cave, it was empty.

Katra found Sasha lying on the beach of the oasis with water lapping over her body. She was weeping. Katra cradled Sasha to her. "There, there, child. Let it all go. Let the healing turquoise waters adsorb the pain so that you can go on to do what you were sent here to do."

Sasha sobbed as she snuggled into Katra's embrace, and the years of pain slowly departed.

- NINE -

Katra and Sasha climbed onto the backs of the pack mules. They had enough supplies to last four days in case the entrances below were "obscured from view," as Katra had said. Katra bowed to her kin that had gathered to see them off.

In the bewitching hour before the sun made its grand appearance on the horizon, the scraggly pup stretched out lazily in deep slumber in the arms of a tall, elderly woman. With miles of desert travel ahead, and then the delicate trekking down the steep, rocky blue ridges, the trip would be far too dangerous for the pup.

"Thank you for watching over him," Sasha said as she wiped away a tear from the corner of her eye. The tall woman only nodded and smiled a toothless grin.

Katra kicked her mule and the two were off amidst whoops and hollers from the villagers, sending up a spiraling dust trail across the desert.

At mid-morning, the sun's rays brutally beat down. Katra halted her mule, and Sasha's followed. Katra pitched a large tent shelter over themselves and the mules. They drank from their canteens and munched on pita bread and chick peas as Katra unpacked the bed rolls and smoothed them out over the soft desert floor.

"Sleep, dear one," Katra said. "We will resume travel once the sun dips low in the sky."

Katra laid down and closed her eyes, but Sasha was restless. Sasha watched the tent billow up and down ever so slightly in the breeze as time drug on. Sasha's birthmark tingled. Something stirred outside their tent, and the mules snorted.

"Katra," Sasha whispered, and Katra awoke.

"Hold still," Katra said, directing her hands heavenward.

A large, burly man with Asian heritage who was dressed with metal plate armor over his chest peered into their tent. He entered with gun pointed, but saw only the mules. He signaled to other men in a strange tongue. The burly man and another came in and took the mules' reins. The girls, invisible, watched the mules be taken away with all of their supplies. Then, the tent was quiet.

"They are watching the tent," Katra whispered.

The burly man came inside and squatted down. He closed his eyes and waited. Sasha held her breath. After what felt like an eternity, he rose and exited the tent. They heard excited voices and horses' hooves and then, silence.

Katra lowered her arms, breaking the cloaking meditation. She quickly stood and peered outside of the tent. Bright moonlight streamed inside in an arc of light.

"They've gone," Katra said as she returned.

Sasha shook as hours of pent-up emotion escaped.

"We are safe now," Katra said as she cradled Sasha in her arms.

"They took everything," Sasha said.

"Don't lose heart," Katra said. "A way will be shone."

Katra began dismantling the tent, scouring the ground for any supplies that may have been overlooked as she went. She tied the tent in a bundle to her back and offered one of the stakes to Sasha as a walking stick.

"Well, the raiding party was thorough," Katra said. "They left nothing."

"Do we turn back?" Sasha asked.

"Not at all," Katra said. "We will hunt for food when we reach the Blue Ridge Mountains. It is a clear night and we haven't far to go."

Katra pointed toward the eastern horizon where a dark ridge rose in the distance against the starlit sky. Spurred on by the proximity of the mountains and the hope of soon reuniting with her sister, the only family she had left, Sasha rose to her feet. The two women set off once more on a journey across the desert.

- TEN -

By mid-morning Katra and Sasha finally reached the great Eastern Blue Ridge Mountains. Sasha drank eagerly from a stream weaving between the rocky ridges and gathered blue berries growing in abundance on its banks. She enjoyed the soothing sound of the trickling stream, and lay back in the soft grass and wildflowers, watching the bright butterflies alight from fragrant blossoms. She giggled as one landed on the tip of her nose.

Katra found an area along the stream sheltered by two ancient weeping willow trees and erected the tent. She sang to the stream, enticing fish to its banks and pulled out two large trout. Sasha gathered kindling from the forest, circling it with a pile of river stones. With a piece of sharp flint, Sasha started a fire beneath the stones as Katra prepared the trout. The women feasted on fish and settled in for some much-needed rest. Meanwhile, deep within the earth, Adrianne was running for her life.

PART 2:

ADRIANNE'S QUANDARY

- ONE -

She hadn't meant to take it. Call it an impulse. The heavy metal box measured two feet across and one foot deep. It was the great nuclear machine that her father had spoken of that should have been tucked safely away, inside a cave within the witch's hat-shaped hill. The Intra-terrestrial beings had stolen it first. She was merely taking it back.

They weren't really using it anyway. The Intra-earth functioned on magnetic frequencies and free ozone energy. She found the nuclear machine on display inside a pyramid museum next to other stolen surface items: automobiles from the early 1900s through mid-2000s, an enormous steam ship, a train with three cars, a set of knight's armor, bronze swords, shields and medieval weaponry, a helicopter, a windmill, early crystal technology prototypes—cell phones and computers, numerous portraits, statues, a jeweled crown, and other obsolete items from the past.

An automated satellite shooting laser darts headed straight for her. Adrianne had made it to the grassy blue cliffs lining the subterranean sea. Where she would go from here, she did not know. "A way will be shone," echoed in her mind. She darted to the side just as a satellite shattered the side of the cliff with its blaster. It wouldn't be the last one. She'd been dodging satellites such as this for the past day and a half. The darn box was getting heavy. She needed to find a place to rest, and fast.

The ravine that she had fallen into that day of the search for the great nuclear machine transported her into another world entirely. Adrianne remembered watching her sister Sasha sobbing on the edge of the cliff. Adrianne focused on her sister's face as she fell so that she would not meet death with fear. . .but then she landed on something soft, white, and buoyant, much like the top of a circus tent.

Adrianne bounced to the ground and found herself surrounded by lush hilltops and people dressed in pastel colors strolling happily among a city of tents. The people resembled those from the Orient. A couple stopped, and the woman smiled and offered her a hand up. The woman spoke in a gentle, unfamiliar tongue, yet she understood. "Welcome, far traveler, you have just entered Mu's Outpost."

Another satellite whizzed towards Adrianne, shaking her back to present time. Her mind must be drifting from lack of food. Adrianne pushed ahead, hugging the rock as she made her way across the narrow path that snaked along the cliffs. There was a thin slit in the cliff face, and she slipped inside. The satellite moved on. The rock was cool, and she momentarily closed her eyes. Suddenly, she was yanked inside the mountain.

Adrianne instinctively raised her hand to her brass hair clip that concealed a tiny, sharp knife. She stood face to face with a gnarly, old woman clothed in rags, and she lowered her hand. The woman spoke in the same strange tongue uttered in Mu, yet, Adrianne understood. "What's such a scrawny crimson-haired thing doing on my threshold?" the old woman asked, but Adrianne remained quiet.

"Ah, you are not from around her? Yes?" the old woman asked. "Such a pretty scarf," the old woman touched the sheer yellow cloth around Adrianne's head, that was held in place by the brass clip. "An offering for using my home?"

Adrianne clung to the scarf but grabbed the bottom of her dress and ripped the lace off at the hem. She handed the lace to the old crone.

"That will do," the woman said. "Have a seat." The woman offered Adrianne a seat on a stone bench in the corner. Something was cooking on the stove, and Adrianne's stomach rumbled.

"You are much too skinny. I will fix you a plate." The woman passed Adrianne a bowl of green gruel, which she devoured.

"The satellites have been active," the woman said. "What do they want with a puny foreigner with crimson tresses?" Adrianne stole a furtive glance at the machine.

"Not your belongings, I gather." The old woman chuckled.

"It will give my people a second chance." Adrianne was too tired to formulate a lie.

"Something wrought by deceit never amounts to good in the end." The old crone chuckled to herself again. "So, I harbor a fugitive, then? Eat your gruel and be off. I am too old for run-ins with Mu law." The woman sat in the back of the cave and rocked back and forth, lightly humming to herself as she ran her fingers over the lace.

"Thank you for the food," Adrianne said, but the old woman ignored her.

Adrianne lifted the box that encased the machine and side-stepped, gingerly maneuvering herself and the heavy box through the narrow slit towards the light. As she exited the crevice in the cliff, she stood face to face with a satellite. A violet-colored laser light shot off of the satellite and zapped her. She was stunned, her whole body immobilized.

Five other satellites zipped towards her. The satellites strung together like beads on a strand, and a large net sprang out, encapsulating her and the box encasing the great nuclear machine. She and the box were lifted into the air and carried over the mountains towards the grand city of Mu.

- ꝡWO -

Sasha slept soundly in the tent beneath the willows. Suddenly, Katra nudged her. "Be very still," Katra whispered.

Something *big* sniffed the tent. The animal stopped behind the tent where Sasha lay and snarled. Sasha screamed. The animal slashed huge claw-marks into the tent, shredding it as Sasha and Katra fled out the other side. The women ran, disappearing into the tree line. Sasha glanced back and saw an enormous male tiger, double the size of a usual Asian tiger, sniffing the air in their direction. The women fled deep into the forest, and then stopped.

"Luckily, the wind's blowing in our favor," Katra said. "We are safe, for now. Come."

Katra led Sasha farther into the forest. They came to an opening, a long expanse of prairie, and in the distance, Sasha spotted the witch's hat-shaped hill. Sasha raced towards the hill and half-way there suddenly dropped to the ground. The tall grass billowed lightly, and the earth stretched seamlessly in front of her. Where was the ravine? There was no trace of where the land had split.

"It's not here," Sasha said. "The ravine. It should be right here."

"Very clever," Katra said as she came up behind Sasha. "They've hidden the entrance. As I'd feared."

"No. It should be right here," Sasha said. "Adrianne," Sasha shouted. "Adrianne!"

"Please, dear one," Katra said. "We will find another way." A branch snapped and the tall grass swayed behind them.

"What is it?" Sasha asked. "The tiger?"

"We must move," Katra said. "To the hill!"

The two women raced through the prairie to the witch's hat-shaped hill. The tiger had picked up their scent and bounded through the grass towards them as the women clambered up to the cave. The tiger was two strides behind. The boulder door easily slid aside and they darted inside, slamming it shut. Katra quickly wedged a stick and rolled a massive rock against the boulder. The tiger collided with the boulder and roared in frustration at losing its meal.

The smell of damp earth and dripping water permeated the women's senses. A single lantern flickered in the back of the cave. "Hello?" Katra called. There was no answer as they warily approached the light. Next to the lantern was a ladder leading below.

- ᵧHREE -

Mu was a city of stone structures and marble colonnades, much like those she'd seen in pictures of the ancient Greek ruins in the land once known as "Italy," smack dab in the center of a dense tropical paradise. Adrianne was lowered down in front of Mu's Parthenon-esque council building. The net retracted into the satellites as they docked around her. She felt suddenly exhausted, and her eyes closed. When she slowly awoke and sat up, the box was gone. All the satellites had disappeared but one; the black-silver satellite glistened at her side.

"We are disappointed in you, far traveler," she felt more than heard in her mind.

Adrianne stood up, and the satellite rose beside her. "That box could have saved my entire civilization!" Adrianne screamed at the empty council courtyard.

"The nuclear machine was the undoing of your civilization," the voice spoke. "By taking it, we prevented further damage and have offered the surface another chance. Life, nature, will return more vivacious than seen in the last twenty-five hundred years."

"I will get it back. You will see," Adrianne challenged.

"That is ill advised," the voice spoke.

"Ahh!" Adrianne screamed, and as she stormed away from the council building, the lone satellite followed. Adrianne stopped, and the satellite stopped. "Go away!" she screamed.

"Satellite 151's mission is to watch girl," the satellite spoke in robotic monotone. "To protect girl from own wrong doings."

"Ahh!" Adrianne screamed again as she stomped down the marble stairs.

- Four -

Through the marble colonnades, the council watched the fiery red-headed girl descend down the steps of the council plaza, shouting obscenities at the satellite.

"She is a most willful child," Elder Matonae spoke.

"Yes, that she is," Elder Aaronlee concurred. He turned to address the council. "She and her sister, like flip sides of the same coin, are strong bridges between our two worlds. Adrianne embodies the fiery passion of the father's blood lineage, and Sasha, the gentle wisdom and powerful intuition of the mother's. The relationships are to be nurtured. Adrianne will bend with time." Elder Aaronlee sighed. "Now, on to more pressing concerns. Surface hostiles that have entered the Intra-earth must be detained and returned to the surface before they reach the borders of our great city."

In a hologram image, the council viewed the burly militants that had stolen provisions from Katra and Sasha, marching towards their beautiful city through the fringes of the expansive tropical forest. But more worrisome than this, was a second hostile war-party from the surface, perched atop a mountain overlooking the city of Mu.

"What of Enoch's colony?" Elder Matonae inquired.

"I fear that they have suffered the worst of fates," Elder Aaronlee stated. "And, with immense sorrow, I must report that Herald's knowledge has been compromised. Those that are encroaching upon our great city are not of pure heart."

"We should dispatch the satellites," Elder Matonae said.

"Yes," Elder Lunatious said.

"At once," Elder Rudoln concurred.

"By unanimous agreement," Elder Aaronlee stated, "the sats are deployed."

The satellites resumed animation, rose, and zipped away from the city, ascending the great mountain that safe-guarded Mu.

- FIVE -

The ladder went down, descending further than the eye could see. Katra began the descent, but Sasha stood back on the threshold, steadying her swirling stomach.

"Grab ahold and climb," Katra said, her voice echoing throughout the cavern.

"It's too far," Sasha said. "We'll never make it." Something outside clawed at the boulder door of the cave. Was it the tiger? Sasha gulped.

"Not if you do not try," Katra said. "Trust, my dear."

Sasha took a deep breath and grabbed ahold of the ladder. Moments after they began the descent, they were suddenly transported to the bottom.

"What happened?" Sasha asked.

"The distance was merely an illusion," Katra said. "We were already on top of the entrance." The women stood on the threshold of a great tropical forest that spanned the horizon, and to the north the blue cliffs dropped down into an expansive ocean. "The size of the forest, however, is not trickery. We have a trek to Mu, the sparkling epicenter of the Intra-earth, where we will, by the grace of the Divine, reunite you with your sister." A large thud came from behind.

"Run!" Katra yelled, and the women dashed into the thick forest.

The enormous tiger stood up, shook itself off, and roared.

- Six -

Adrianne emerged from the stairs of the council building and made a sharp left. The satellite zipped towards her. "This is the wrong course," the satellite quipped. "Turn around. Girl is off course. Girl must return to her dormitory, at once."

Ah, her dormitory. A white tent, identical to the others, perched at the end of the village. It was nice, she wouldn't lie. Not much to see from the outside, but within was quite spacious and bright, with a comfortable sleep mat, a cushy chair and table, a closet full of clothes from many eras, early millennial books and movies from the surface, complete with a pre-historic DVD and record player, all stolen from the surface, she'd guessed. She was bored. . .and she missed Sasha.

Adrianne sped up, but the robot only swooped closer, harping at her. She squatted down and scooped up a handful of pebbles which she launched at the satellite. The satellite zipped to the side, narrowly missing impact. "If you do not alter your course, at once, satellite 151 will alter it for you," the satellite warned.

Adrianne sighed and turned towards her dormitory. The satellite happily buzzed behind her. A couple strolling by nodded to her, and she nodded back. The people here were kind, but distant. And where were the kids? She hadn't seen one person under the age of 25 since arriving in Mu.

Suddenly, Adrianne charged the robot, shoving it into a tree, and took off. The satellite rose and zipped after her at full speed. A violet-colored laser light shot off of the robot and zapped her. Adrianne lay in a stunned heap on the ground. The last thing she saw was the robot hover above her before she closed her eyes.

- SEVEN -

Adrianne awoke, lying on the sleep mat inside her dormitory tent. The satellite sat, inert, beside her bed. Adrianne stood and began rummaging around the tent. She went to an ancient safe vault and cranked the handle. The handle spun and then the door to the vault swung open, revealing entertainment from centuries past. She pulled out a television with a DVD player on the bottom. She grinned as she had only read about these. She pushed the play button and the ancient classic, *Harry Potter and the Sorcerer's Stone*, began.

Adrianne paused the scene where Harry was an infant and attacked by Voldemort, forming the scar on his forehead. She plopped down on her sleep mat and opened a dusty *Popular Mechanics* magazine. "How to rewire a circuit," was the title of the article. Adrianne un-paused the movie, and with Harry's adventures in Hogwarts in the background, she read about the proper wiring to use, the loop that electricity must travel, grounding wires, connecting conductors. . . and dozed off.

Hours later, Adrianne stirred and the movie was over. She cranked open the vault, preparing to select yet another movie and magazine. The satellite remained inert. She sighed. "Great company, you are," Adrianne said to the satellite, but it only just sat there.

Adrianne rose and headed for the flap of cloth that functioned as a door. Instantly, the satellite revived and zipped towards her.

"Well, there you are," Adrianne said as the satellite hovered in front of her, blocking the exit.

"Girl cannot leave," the satellite said. "First disobedience results in detainment in dormitory."

"First disobedience?" Adrianne smirked. "What happens the second time?"

"Second disobedience results in detainment in council chamber. Third disobedience results in chemical therapy. Fourth disobedience results in personality restructure."

"Oh, Lord on Zion's Mount," Adrianne said. "And these people think we are backwards."

"Backwards. . .not in Satellite 151's data base," the satellite spoke as it scrolled through its programming.

"How long am I detained?" Adrianne demanded.

"Until girl deemed not dangerous," the satellite said.

"That is ridiculous," Adrianne said. "I am dangerous for trying save my entire civilization?"

"Girl must not attempt to retrieve the machine."

"My name's Adrianne," she said. "Move."

"Girl, Adrianne, must not attempt to retrieve the machine," the satellite repeated.

Adrianne appeared to back down. She turned to go to her bed, and the satellite lowered. Suddenly, Adrianne leapt onto the table beside her sleep mat and launched herself at the satellite, side-kicking it into the entertainment vault. She flew at the vault and slam-cranked the handle, locking the satellite inside. Clanging and booming rang from the vault as the satellite rammed into its sides.

"I will take my chances with a second disobedience," Adrianne said before dashing from the tent.

- EIGHT -

The soldiers from the surface set up a base camp in the great Intra-earth jungle on a mountaintop overlooking the city of Mu. They were a motley band of nomads, renegade fighters, and mercenaries. The leader, dressed in a silk thobe with a massive gun strapped to his chest, was unassuming in appearance except for his quick, steel-colored eyes that looked through you. The leader, holding a round metallic disc, watched the city, waiting.

A dark silver cloud ascended from the city below. As it got closer, the satellites came into view. The satellites swooped low over the base camp, firing violet laser-like darts. The men scattered. A few were struck by the lasers and laid on the ground, stunned. The leader activated the disc in his hand, and it lifted into the sky.

"Lie low!" the leader shouted.

The men leapt to the ground and covered their ears. The disc zipped up and emitted a high-pitched sonar frequency and a whip of energy spiraled off of the metallic disc. Suddenly, all of the satellites fell from the sky.

The leader rose to his feet and walked over to a fallen satellite. It lay still and had a dented-in side from impact. The leader opened a panel on the back of the satellite and crossed wires. The satellite rose and hovered over his shoulder.

The men gathered around the leader. "Bring in any salvageable machines," he ordered.

The soldiers went to work, pushing, pulling and dragging in the satellites, which were rewired in turn. Slowly, the satellites rose behind the soldiers, adding another string to their battalion.

"We strike at nightfall," the leader commanded.

"Sir?" a nomad inquired. "The sun never sets in this land beneath the crust."

"Then, we strike now!" the leader shouted.

The men roared with approval as they climbed onto their steeds and began the descent down the mountaintop towards Mu.

- NINE -

As Katra and Sasha raced into the dense subterranean tropical forest, they were by no means alone. The two war parties that they had passed early on in their adventure, one being the band of fearsome nomads that had marched past Katra's oasis village, and the other one they had encountered in the desert, were also rapidly encroaching upon the city of Mu.

Katra stopped and listened. It was quiet, except for the steady hum of insects and cackling birds. She directed Sasha to a tall tree, and the women climbed. Once in the crook of the thick branches, they rested.

Katra startled awake. She surveyed the land below. Lush greenery spanned the horizon. There was no sign of the tiger, but she did see rising smoke half a kilometer to the east.

"Is that Mu?" Sasha inquired.

"I am not certain," Katra said, "but, my hunch is that it is someone that came down before us. Many, by the look of the smoke plumes."

"Why are you risking your life to help me?" Sasha asked quietly. "You have your village around the oasis—"

"It is my duty," Katra replied, and Sasha looked away.

"Our destinies are entwined. . . yet, it is more. . . I imagine that my own daughter would have been much like you." Katra's eyes glistened. "She was taken from me when she was just a baby, delivered into the arms of the Great Creator on the same day as my beloved." Katra sighed. "That was a long time ago, before I came upon the oasis."

"I am so sorry." Sasha sniffled, stifling a sob.

"Don't be sad," Katra said as she placed a hand to her chest. "It finally brings my heart peace to aid you on your path."

Men screamed three hundred yards away from their tree, and the tiger roared.

"We will give the tiger and the invaders a wide berth," Katra said as she wiped the moisture from her eyes. "Come, we best make haste."

Sasha shimmied down the tree trunk after Katra.

- TEN -

Inside Adrianne's dormitory tent, Satellite 151 shot its blasters. The lid of the vault flew off, and the satellite soared out of the vault. The satellite swiveled around and incinerated the vault with its blasters before zipping from the tent.

- $\mathcal{E}$LEVEN -

Adrianne snaked into the pyramid-shaped Museum of Ancient Antiquities. She tip-toed past rows of ancient automobiles, bicycles, and boats. Through aisles of books, magazines, and movies she dashed. She ended up circling rooms of statues, paintings, and abstract art until she found the room of technology. After rows of computers and outdated steam and gasoline engines, there it was, the great nuclear machine. She laughed with relief. She hoisted it up and bounded towards the exit.

Adrianne lunged out of the building and into the open air. The courtyard was deserted. Where was everyone? No matter. She had one mission: to get this machine to the surface. Adrianne headed in the direction of the blue cliffs where she first fell into this mythical world.

- ᏣWELVE -

Mu's Council Elders, seeing the failure of their satellites, began the next course of action: evacuation of their great city. Mu was a flourishing center of art and culture, not a war state. Chaos engulfed the city as the elders directed people to the space station or to the tunnel system that linked intra-terrestrial nations. Heavy gates encompassing the city were raised to bide them time.

Gongs rang out as the soldiers breached the gates, the leader with steel eyes at the helm. The satellites zipped ahead, stunning any wayfaring citizens. The leader ascended the steps to the council building and was pleased to find it empty.

"An easy victory!" the leader shouted from the summit.

The soldiers cheered.

"Enjoy the plenitude of your new home!" the leader shouted. "We shall name it Tartan, in honor of my fallen brethren!"

In the distance, beyond the roaring crowd, a girl with red hair carrying a box scurried past.

"Stop her," the leader commanded, and the satellites rose. "Bring her to me." The satellites took flight.

Adrianne saw the sats approaching and raced full fledge ahead, but they overtook her.

"You are surrounded," a satellite stated. "Proceed to the Supreme Leader."

Adrianne allowed herself to be led towards the council building by the swarming satellites, when suddenly she changed course. She set the box down and leapt from the box onto a satellite. She rode on the satellite, pounding it as it spun around, weaving to and fro. The wobbling satellite shot lasers, zapping other satellites, which careened to the ground.

The satellite finally shook Adrianne off, and she landed with a hard thud onto the ground. A satellite was instantly atop of her and zapped her with violet light. Three satellites strung together, netted her, and carried her back to the leader. One satellite carried the box in a net. She and the box were delivered to the bottom stairs of the council building.

When she came to, the crowd was gone. Seated on the council steps, next to the box, was the leader with the steel-colored eyes.

"Hello, Adrianne," the leader said.

"I don't know who you are," Adrianne said. "But that box belongs to me. Give it back."

"I am Tartarus." He chuckled. "You've got fighting spirit. Expected of my daughter."

"Uh-uh," Adrianne said. "You are *not* my father."

Tartarus lifted a lock of hair from his forehead and near his hair-line was the same red diamond birthmark as her sister. "I am your father. Remember, Adrianne."

Tartarus touched his temple, and Adrianne felt her

brain tingle as her vision became fuzzy. An image floated into her consciousness of her as a baby in Tartarus's arms. He was different; younger, happier. Sasha as a toddler held his hand and giggled as she kissed Adrianne's infant cheek. The girls' mother wrapped her arms around them all, and the image dissolved.

"A pity about your mother. Thank you for delivering the machine," Tartarus said as he rose. "Saves time. Though I have little use for it here—"

"You don't understand," Adrianne said. "I need the machine to save our civilization—"

"My civilization," Tartarus yawned. "They were dying a slow death. The malfunctioning of the great machines only sped up the process."

Tartarus turned and ascended the stairs to the council building with the box.

"Wait!" Adrianne screamed as she flew up the stairs after him. Tartarus spun around and she saw that there was no light in his eyes, only death. He raised his hand.

"Unfortunately, I have no use for a daughter either. Dispose of her," Tartarus commanded, and he disappeared inside the building.

Five satellites rose and headed for Adrianne. Red lasers fired, and Adrianne shut her eyes. When she opened them, the five satellites were lying on the ground in a haze of electrical smoke. A satellite emerged from the foliage and Adrianne jumped.

"Girl, Adrianne, Satellite 151 must protect," the satellite said as it hovered closer, lowering a platform from its base.

"I owe you one." Adrianne embraced the satellite.

"Girl, Adrianne, get on platform at once," the satellite said.

Adrianne climbed onto the platform, and she and the satellite soared off over the great forest.

Part 3:
The Revelation

- ONE -

Katra and Sasha trekked through the thick jungle, giving the tiger and the invading party's camp plenty of space. Something jingled in the distance and Katra raised her hand, signaling Sasha to halt. Two mules galloped past, and Katra grabbed ahold of the lead mule's reins and jumped onto its back, slowing the other. The ornate emblem of Katra's kin shined from the mules' bridles.

"Aren't these your animals?" Sasha asked.

"Yes." Katra gleamed. "They've returned to us, and they are still carrying provisions. A blessing, indeed!" Katra stroked the mules' necks.

"Do you think they were spooked by the tiger?" Sasha asked.

"Very possibly," Katra agreed. "Let's put a wide berth between us and the fearsome beast."

Sasha climbed onto the other mule's back, and the women pushed ahead through the jungle toward the grand city of Mu. Obscured from view by thick jungle canopy, they failed to see Adrianne and the satellite fly over them.

- Two -

The satellite zipped low over the great tropical forest, taking cover beneath the branches of the thick canopy when the cloud of the Supreme Leader's satellites swarmed close. When all danger had passed, the satellite lifted above the canopy, resuming flight with Adrianne as passenger. A tiger roared from below. The satellite continued until reaching the blue cliffs. The turquoise sea rhythmically lapped against the bottom of the cliffs, sending up a frothy spray, lulling Adrianne off to sleep.

After hours of travel, they reached the opening in the cliff with the ladder. The ladder appeared to rise up forever. The satellite zipped up the optical illusion and into the cave. The lantern at the top of the ladder had been knocked over and the light was snuffed out. A boulder with large claw marks half blocked the cave opening. The satellite shot its laser-blasters at the boulder, obliterating the rock, and zipped from the cave. The sun was just appearing on the horizon, and Adrianne yawned as she awoke. She glanced behind and saw the witch's hat-shaped hill, and her memory stirred.

"Wait," Adrianne said.

The satellite stopped, hovering in midair. "Girl,

Adrianne, is awake?"

"Yes. Stop, please," Adrianne said.

"Not safe to stop," the satellite quipped as it continued on its trajectory. "Satellite 151's mission is to protect girl. Mu's Satellite Fleet had lethal settings activated. Mu's Satellite Fleet is to protect and serve, not to kill. Satellite 151 finds this most alarming."

Adrianne suddenly jumped off of the platform, hit the prairie floor and tumbled. She lay splayed out on the ground and the satellite buzzed around her, scanning her for injury.

"Knock it off," Adrianne said. "I am fine." She laughed and stood up. "You really are a pest."

Adrianne watched the satellite scroll its database as images of pests: wasps, flies, ants, and other insects formed in front of the satellite on a holographic screen. "Just joking around," she said. Images of termites, snakes, and spiders flashed across the screen. "Wow, you are literal. Stop," Adrianne said.

The satellite ceased scrolling its database and emitted a laser-light over the landscape, scanning its surroundings. A streak of tigers had just picked up their scent and stalked near, while just beyond the blue ridge, soldiers approached from the west through the desert. The satellite hovered squarely in front of Adrianne. "Girl, Adrianne, must get on platform at once," the satellite said. "Danger—"

"I need some answers first," Adrianne said as she stepped back.

"No time," the satellite said and bumped into Adrianne, catching her off guard. Adrianne fell sideways onto the satellite's platform as it flew up. Suddenly, three enormous tigers leapt from the grass, clawing for her. Adrianne screamed as she hung from the platform.

Adrianne climbed onto the platform, and the satellite altered its course, heading back to the hill shaped like a witch's hat.

- THREE -

The satellite fired lasers at the top of the hill shaped like a witch's hat, creating a landslide of boulders, before disappearing inside the cave. The boulders crashed down, blocking the exit. The satellite emitted laser light, lighting torches throughout the cave. Adrianne hopped off of the platform.

"I need answers, now," Adrianne demanded.

"Yes, it is time. Girl, Adrianne, must know the truth," the satellite stated as it hovered beside her.

A hologram image projected from the satellite. Adrianne saw herself and Sasha as young children next to their mother and Tartarus as one happy family. Her mother and Tartarus looked very much in love. The image changed to Tartarus gaining power in the council and after each political victory, his heart grew colder with ambition and greed. Her mother and Tartarus increasingly fought.

Tartarus, in secret, killed a rival, taking his place in the Jadeneize High Council. Their mother suspected this and reported this to the High Elders, forcing Tartarus to flee Jadeneize. After this betrayal, their mother sought solace with a very old friend, Tanner, the man the girls knew as father. The hologram diminished, and Adrianne collapsed to her knees.

"So, it is true," Adrianne said. "That monster is my father."

"That is affirmative," the satellite said.

"And he has the machine," Adrianne said.

"Affirmat—" the satellite began.

"You're going to help me get it back," Adrianne interjected.

"Satellite 151's mission is to protect girl, Adrianne," the satellite said as it scrolled its database. "Too many variables. Probability of successful recovery of nuclear machine is 12, no, 8%. Safer course, is to keep girl, Adrianne, hidden."

"I don't think so," Adrianne said as she made for the ladder.

"Wait, girl, Adrianne," the satellite said as it continued to scroll its database. "There is more. . ."

Adrianne paused atop the ladder.

"Your mother is alive, but struggles on the surface. She is in a very dark place," the satellite spoke. "Sasha is in danger. She is nearly to Mu's gates. In search of you."

"Well," Adrianne said, brushing away a stubborn tear coursing down her cheek, "we best hurry, then." She leapt off of the ladder and into the land beneath. Satellite 151 swiveled around and blasted the walls of the cavern, creating a landslide that sealed the portal between the two worlds, before zipping down after her.

- Four -

Within Mu's spacious council building, all of the council's sparkling and jeweled, high-backed chairs had been removed, but one. Tartarus reclined on his throne with two satellite sentinels hovering at his sides. He sneered at the large marble sculptures of Greek gods and goddesses that surrounded him: to his right, Lady Athena held an owl in her outstretched palm. Behind him, rose Zeus with his fiery lightning bolt, and to his left, the goddess Themis wielded her sword and tipped scale.

"Gods of old, give witness to me, the new Supreme Leader," Tartarus decreed. "Soon, I shall have dominion over all of Earth."

The chamber doors opened, and a third satellite buzzed in. Seconds later, a burly, armed militant entered. The satellite took its place behind Tartarus.

"You summoned me, my Lord," the militant said.

"Ah, yes," Tartarus said. "Give the girl a proper burial."

"My Lord?" the militant asked.

"You are excused." Tartarus waved his hand dismissively.

"What girl?" the militant asked.

"The girl who is toast at the bottom of the steps!" Tartarus roared.

"There's no girl," the militant stated. "Only five downed satellites." Tartarus clenched the metallic disc in his lap, and the satellites rose and pointed their glowing, red laser blasters at the militant.

"My Lord, we were hunting down the council," the militant explained. "There's no girl. Please, my Lord," he begged, but Tartarus lifted the disc and the three satellites fired their blasters. The militant dropped.

Tartarus descended the steps to the fallen satellites. They were riddled with large holes bored by lasers. One by one, he lifted the back panels from the machines, but the inside circuits were fried. All but one. Tartarus skillfully restored life to the last satellite, and it rose to his side.

"What happened to the girl?" Tartarus demanded.

The satellite replayed the battle on its projector, and Tartarus saw Adrianne rescued by Satellite 151.

"Locate Satellite 151," Tartarus ordered, and the satellite began scrolling.

- FIVE -

Sasha and Katra slept beneath a purple sky deep within the subterranean jungle. They rested comfortably on bedrolls with bellies full from the mules' provisions, while the mules grazed beside them. Lights flashed in the distance. Within the grand city of Mu, a second war had waged with a victor already crowned.

Tartarus lowered the metallic disc and the satellite guardians ascended up the council steps to the inner chambers, taking their position behind the Supreme Leader. The grounds of Mu lay splayed with the bodies of the fallen invaders. One, not quite dead, was netted by a satellite and dropped at Tartarus' feet. The burly invader dressed in plate armor stirred.

"To whom do I owe the pleasure?" Tartarus asked, but the burly invader only sputtered and coughed. "Speak now, or die," Tartarus ordered.

The man spoke, but it was in an unfamiliar tongue. Tartarus lifted the disc and the satellites pointed their laser blasters at the invader. The invader got down to one knee, obviously begging for his life.

"Translate," Tartarus said.

"The intruder is Neatuke from the Miazooki Clan, from

the far north, in the vicinity of Lake Xau," Satellite 263 spoke in robotic monotone. "Those of the Miazooki Clan that survived the malfunctioning were taken as slaves by a stronger clan. All that remain fight at his side, until they win back the rest. His clans' last hope for survival lies in the folkloric tales of the Intra-earth. He pledges his life in servitude to you, Supreme Leader."

"We aren't recruiting," Tartarus said as he raised the disc. Satellite 263 fired its laser blasters, and Neatuke dropped.

- Six -

Satellite 151 zipped just beneath the canopy of the great Intra-earth jungle, weaving between the massive trunks. Adrianne groaned from the platform below. Satellite 151 dipped to the forest floor.

"What are we doing?" Adrianne demanded.

"Girl, Adrianne, needs nourishment," the satellite said as it docked near a grove of peach and almond trees.

Adrianne was too hungry to put up a fight. She leapt off of the platform and snatched a juicy peach from a low hanging branch and feasted ravenously, while Satellite 151 zipped up to the high tops of the almond trees to harvest ripe clusters. Adrianne threw the peach pit and pulled the branch lower, reaching for another. Suddenly, she came face to face with an enormous, nightmarish tiger. Crouching down, the beast still towered over her.

Adrianne reached behind her head to the brass hair clip and unsheathed a tiny knife. The tiger leapt from behind the peach tree. Adrianne rolled across the ground and then bolted up, squarely holding the beast's gaze, with knife poised. The two danced around each other, until the tiger bolted off into the thicket. Satellite 151 realized Adrianne's danger too late. The satellite zipped down from the high branches with firey laser-blasters drawn, just as the tiger vanished into the thick foliage.

"Where were you?" Adrianne demanded as she returned the knife to its brass clip. "I was nearly tiger-lunch!"

"Satellite 151 was procuring food for girl, Adrianne." The satellite shined a cluster of ripe almonds with its laser-blasters on low, drying them, and then presented the cluster to Adrianne. She pertly snatched the perfect almonds and stuffed them into her mouth.

"There are no large predatory felines native to this forest," the satellite said as it madly scrolled its databases.

"Aww, is the orb perplexed?" Adrianne smirked.

The satellite proceeded to scan Adrianne for injury as it lowered its platform.

"Quit it," Adrianne said. "I am fine."

"You are the responsibility of Satellite 1-5—"

"What kind of a name is 1-5-1?" she said as she leisurely reclined onto the platform. "How about I call you, Orbie?"

"Or-bie?" The satellite inquired as it ascended to the tree tops.

- SEVEN -

As Satellite 151, carrying Adrianne as passenger, ascended above the canopy, six satellites in the command of the Supreme Leader immediately surrounded them on all sides with red, lethal blasters activated and pointed. Satellite 151 used all of its defenses to encase Adrianne in a protective magnetic field. Blasters were fired and Satellite 151 dropped. Adrianne screamed as they crashed through the jungle.

They landed hard and rolled across the forest floor.

"Girl, Adrianne. . ." Satelite 151 zapped and crackled with electrical smoke. "Run. The S-satellites are advancing—"

"No! Orbie!" Adrianne screamed as the magnetic field flickered and dissipated.

"Self-destruct sequence initiated." Orbie began counting down as Adrianne fled, racing blindly into the thick moss and towering prehistoric ferns that blanketed the forest floor.

A large fiery blast ignited at her back.

- $\mathcal{E}$IGHT -

A fleet of satellites soared above, entering the grand city of Mu, as Katra and Sasha neared the tall wall encasing the city. Under thick cover of the Intra-earth forest, the women dismounted. Katra grabbed two packs off of the mules and tossed one to Sasha. The mules brayed and trotted towards a grassy meadow to graze, while Katra and Sasha warily proceeded in the direction of the high city gates.

There was no guard at the gates to offer passage. Katra removed a rope from her pack, and the women climbed the wall to the cobblestone causeway above, but also found it empty. Beyond the walls, there wasn't a soul. "It's as I feared," Katra whispered as she motioned to Sasha to get down. "The war parties made it here first." Katra pointed to the armed militants standing guard outside Mu's High Council Building.

Suddenly, three satellites rose from the council building, soaring in their direction.

"Run!" Katra said. "We can cloak ourselves from the men, but not from the sats!"

- NINE -

Adrianne fled deep into the jungle. A mechanical whirring filled her ears as the satellites dipped low in search of her. She mucked through a swamp and hid between the massive, hollow logs and floating debris. She heard a snarl in the distance, and one satellite crashed down. That was the last that she heard from the satellites. Amidst the swamp's sorry symphony of frogs and cicadas, tears fell that wouldn't quit.

A branch cracked, and Adrianne was snapped out of her misery. Low breathing came from behind. Adrianne grabbed a large stick as a bludgeon and leapt from the water, coming face to face with the fearsome tiger. As they circled each other, she caught a glimpse of holes bored into the tiger's ears. The tiger roared, and Adrianne roared back. The tiger peered at the small, fiery woman ready to strike, and then bounded deep into the foliage.

Adrianne dropped the stick and collapsed to her knees. The tiger reappeared, and Adrianne gasped as she slowly reached to withdraw the knife from her brass hair clip. The beast nudged a large hare towards her. The tiger sat back on its haunches and waited.

- TEN -

Sasha's birthmark tingled as the two women raced down the cobblestone road on top of the wall, searching for cover. The satellites would soon be upon them. Suddenly, Sasha knew where to go. "Under the wall!" she shouted.

The wall bridged over a wide stream. Sasha yanked up a hidden hatched door in the road, revealing stairs leading down to the water. Katra and Sasha slipped inside, closing the hatch-door behind them. The satellites zipped over the wall and continued on past.

- $\mathcal{E}$LEVEN -

Within Mu's Council Building, Tartarus reclined on the throne with three black-silver satellites behind him. The metallic disc rested in his lap. A satellite buzzed down the long corridor towards his throne, and he yawned.

"Satellite 263, loyal servant of the Supreme Leader, has successfully recovered the memory cell of Satellite 151," the satellite spoke as it hovered before Tartarus. A compartment opened in the body of the satellite, and it extended a robotic arm which grasped a circuit panel.

"Access it," Tartarus ordered.

The robotic arm drew the circuit panel back into Sat 263's body, and an image formed above the satellite. It was of Adrianne and Satellite 151 inside the cavern within the witch's hat-shaped hill. The image replayed.

"Wait, girl, Adrianne," Satellite 151 said as it continued to scroll its database. "There is more. . ."

Adrianne paused atop the ladder.

"Your mother is alive, but struggles on the surface. She is in a very dark place," Satellite 151 spoke. "Sasha is in danger. She is nearly to Mu's gates. In search of you." The image became hazy.

A transmission came through on Tartarus' wrist

communication device. It was one of the militants guarding Mu's Council Building.

"Supreme Leader, two beings, we think women, were spotted on the wall. The sats were released, but they returned with no intel," the militant stated.

"This is about to get interesting," Tartarus said as he ended the transmission.

- TWELVE -

Sasha and Katra descended down the stone steps to the water.

"Do you wonder how I knew about the secret door in the wall?" Sasha asked.

"Not at all," Katra said. "You are both a Daughter of the House of Jeneva and a Daughter of the House of Tartan."

"Not Tartan," Sasha said. "I am a Daughter of the Houses of Jeneva and Minewaa."

"Hmm," Katra said. "I feel that your true identity has been hidden from you for your protection. It is your birthmark that reveals who you are, my dear."

Sasha quietly followed Katra into the water. Arguing her true identity would be futile.

"The water throws off the sats' thermal scanners," Katra said. "We will travel by stream until we reach the outlying settlements. There, we may find allies. Adrianne, I fear, is no longer here."

"Yes, she is," Sasha insisted as she reached up to soothe her tingling birthmark. Suddenly, Sasha climbed out of the stream.

The black cloud of satellites loomed near.

"Sasha, wait!" Katra called.

Sasha dashed along the wall heading back towards the high city gates.

PART 4:
THE RECKONING

- ONE -

Adrianne stood outside of the tall gates of Mu with the tiger at her side. The tiger's ears moved slightly, and she once again noted the holes; it was a common practice to pierce the ears of tigers that served the far-eastern sovereign. A cluster of satellites flew over, and she hunkered down beneath the fronds of a giant fern, while the tiger stood its ground in the open. A satellite paused midair in the sky and scanned the tiger.

"Sat 98 resume formation at once," hissed over the radio communication. Sat 98 fired red laser-bursts at the tiger, narrowly missing him, before zipping over the wall and into the city of Mu.

More satellites flew over the wall as the tiger paced.

"We need a plan," Adrianne said to herself as she emerged from hiding. "Sats are patrolling the wall too close."

Suddenly the tiger grabbed the bunch of loose cloth gathered at the nape of Adrianne's neck and ran with the tiny girl. A guard emerged from a concealed doorway in the wall. The guard startled at seeing the massive cat and raised his weapon. In one movement the tiger tossed Adrianne to the side and pounced the guard. Adrianne landed lightly on her feet.

The tiger sat back on his haunches and waited.

"Well done, my hairy friend." Adrianne stroked the tiger's chest. "We'll work on the carriage." The tiger bounded after Adrianne through the open doorway in the wall and into the grand city of Mu.

- TWO -

Racing along the wall, Sasha collided with a girl that emerged from a concealed doorway in the wall. *Adrianne!* The sisters tearfully embraced as time was at a standstill. An enormous tiger emerged.

"No!" Katra screamed as she ran paces behind Sasha. Katra immediately raised an arm, concealing herself and the girls in a shroud of invisibility as the tiger paced. The cluster of satellites were upon them, viewing the three women and the tiger with their infrared scanners.

"Run!" Katra yelled.

The satellites' laser-blasters fired, riddling the ground before the tiger.

The women watched as the tiger leapt up and batted at the satellites, catching one. The satellite careened into another and they both exploded on the ground. More satellites fired their laser-blasters as the tiger attacked. The tiger destroyed two more satellites, until a third dealt a heavy blow. The tiger rolled across the ground and then was still.

"No!" Adrianne screamed as she faced the satellites.

The satellites stunned and netted the three women and lifted them, forwarding them to the destiny that awaited within the council building.

- THREE -

Adrianne and Sasha awoke within their netted prison that soared above the grand city of Mu, and clasped hands. Katra lay still between them.

"I saw you fall. . .I thought you were dead," Sasha whispered as a heavy tear escaped, coursing a pathway down her cheek.

"Never." Adrianne smiled. "Mother?" she inquired.

Sasha shook her head.

"We will bring her back," Adrianne said with unyielding conviction.

Sasha looked away. How could she tell Adrianne that their mother had died trying to save her?

"No," Adrianne said, instinctively knowing what her sister was thinking. "She's alive."

Sasha met Adrianne's eyes that burned bright.

"I missed you," Sasha mouthed the words.

Tartarus applauded as the women were delivered in their netted prisons and dropped before his throne. "A grand spectacle, indeed," Tartarus said. "Adrianne, it appears that you are like one of your little cats, having multiple lives. Utterly obsessed with this useless machine." The great nuclear machine rested at his feet. "If you behave yourselves, I may remove the nets."

"Unhand me, you barbarian!" Adrianne screamed.

"Tsk, tsk," Tartarus said. "Do not test me, darling." Tartarus lifted the gold disc in his lap, and the satellites pointed their glowing, red laser-blasters at the women.

Adrianne met her sister's eyes. "He believes that he is our father," the message formed in Sasha's mind as she studied the stranger on the throne.

"You doubt me?" Tartarus sneered as he ran his hand through his hair, revealing the birthmark that mirrored the one between Sasha's eyes.

Sasha gasped.

"Yes, quite a coincidence, indeed," he said.

"I don't care who you are!" Sasha said. "Adrianne risked her life for that machine."

"The machine is the rightful possession of the ruling Minewaa House!" Adrianne shouted.

"Yes," Tartarus said. "When they arrive, maybe I will give it to them. Maybe. Oh, probably not. The Minewaa, the Jeneva, they can all die as far as I am concerned. Tartan is the new ruling class. Join, or be extinguished." Tartarus depressed a button on the arm of the throne, and the nuclear machine descended into a compartment in the floor, with the thick stone floor resealing atop of it.

"These are your children!" Katra exclaimed.

"None I raised," Tartarus said.

"By blood!" Katra said.

"Silence," Tartarus said as he clenched a fist, and Katra clasped her neck and dropped.

"What did you do to her!" Sasha screamed.

"I am so merciful I could vomit," Tartarus said. "Join, or not join. Your answer decides your fate."

"Never!" the girls shouted in unison.

"I will enjoy your demise," Tartarus said as he lifted the disc. His three sentinel satellites rose to his side with red laser-blasters pointed.

From outside the chamber came the sound of satellites crashing down. Someone screamed. The doors flew open. The massive tiger, though wounded, with laser marks staining its beautiful hide, charged down the corridor.

"Stop him," Tartarus ordered, lifting the disc.

Satellites streamed into the chamber, surrounding the tiger on all sides. The tiger hunkered down.

"Kill it!" Tartarus commanded.

As the satellites zeroed in on the tiger and fired their blasters, the tiger leapt into the air. The satellites lifted up, trying to follow their target. Their laser-blasts zapped three satellites, and the injured satellites swiveled and smoked, riddling laser-fire as they whirled. More satellites were struck. The tiger kicked the sparking satellites towards the throne.

The three satellite sentinels retracted the nets from the girls and descended upon the tiger as Adrianne and Sasha, dodging fallen satellites, bounded down the long corridor towards the exit doors.

The satellite sentinels fired their blasters. The tiger dashed left and right, evading the deathly blasts, with the satellites in close pursuit. The tiger suddenly altered its course, bounded into the air with a large paw raised, and swiped a satellite. The satellite ricocheted into the second satellite sentinels' laser-fire and both careened haphazardly down the hall.

Adrianne and Sasha crouched low as the damaged satellites crashed over. The second satellite sentinel regained its bearing and lifted, facing the tiger with lethal blasters pointed. Adrianne attacked by surprise, racing and bounding off of the wall as she unsheathed her hidden knife. She landed upon the satellite, and riding the spinning orb, gouged her knife beneath its rear control panel. The satellite sputtered, smoked, and plummeted in a downward spiral. Pulling out her knife, she jumped off, and the girls ran until finally reaching the doors.

From the throne, Tartarus raised his arm in the air. The exit doors slammed shut, and the girls were trapped inside. He clenched his fist and gripped the girls' necks, dragging them back to him.

The tiger nicked another satellite, and it spun into a wall. The satellite ignited on impact, and the tiger batted the fiery ball towards the throne. The tiger barreled down the corridor behind the satellite. As Tartarus stepped away from the throne, avoiding the fiery satellite, the tiger leapt at him. A third satellite sentinel emerged from behind the cover of the throne and fired its blasters.

"No!" Adrianne screamed as her tiger was hit. The tiger fell in a heavy heap upon Tartarus. The girls sputtered and coughed as his grip upon their necks was released. Adrianne tried to rise and go to her tiger.

Suddenly, Sasha clasped onto Adrianne's hand.

"We need to go!" Sasha screamed.

Statues of the Greek gods surrounded the throne. Sasha lunged to the right, and reaching up, yanked down the side of the goddess Themis' scale, balancing the weights. A hidden chamber emerged from behind the throne, illuminated with blue flames lining the walls that led deeper within the council building. The girls dashed inside.

Staggering, Tartarus emerged in front the doorway to the hidden entrance and formed a tight fist. The girls wheezed and sputtered as they were drawn back to the Supreme Leader.

"One final chance you are being offered, to bear allegiance to the Supreme Leader." Tartarus grimaced. "So very simple, really."

The third and final satellite sentinel fled down the corridor towards the exit, drawing Tartarus' gaze.

The enormous tiger rose from beside the throne and leapt at the Supreme Leader. Tartarus turned and looked in fear upon the massive tiger flying through the air, clawing for him, clasped the disc, and suddenly, vanished.

The tiger collapsed next to the burning throne.

Adrianne and Sasha raced back through the hidden corridor.

"Good kitty." Adrianne hugged her tiger companion as he weakly purred.

"We made it!" Sasha dropped to her knees with laughter and tears. "You are really here!" She threw her arms around her sister, and spattered kisses upon her cheeks. "Oh, Great One, how we have been blessed!"

"Yes, sister," Adrianne agreed with glee. "It wasn't my time. As you know, there is a Divine plan—"

"Well done, my dears," Katra said as she came to.

"You're alive!" Sasha embraced Katra, who had become a most precious friend.

"Mu must be restored to its former glory." Katra shook as she saw the tiger, but relaxed as she saw Adrianne stroking the beast's head. "I surmise that we had more than a little assistance from the animal kingdom?"

- $\mathcal{F}$OUR -

With the tyrant removed, the people and its council returned to the grand city of Mu. Adrianne, Sasha, and Katra stood before Aaronlee, the preeminent leader of the council.

Adrianne hoisted up the box with the great nuclear machine.

"We are indebted to you, Daughters of the Houses of Jeneva and Tartan, for restoring peace in Mu," Elder Aaronlee spoke. "Therefore, we will gift you with the great nuclear machine. It shall be the undoing of your civilization, yet it is yours."

"There are so many in suffering," Adrianne said.

"Yes, it will bring immediate relief," Elder Aaronlee stated, "but nothing sustainable. Return when you are ready to learn of more long-term energy sources. Katra has agreed to stay amongst us and study magnetics and free ozone energy. We hopefully await your return."

Sasha and Adrianne descended the steps of Mu's council building carrying the great nuclear machine. The Council of Elders watched the girls' descent.

"Did we do the right thing by giving them the machine?" Elder Matonae inquired.

"It is time for the surface races to be their own saviors," Elder Aaronlee stated. "Only then may they take their proper place among the Intra-planetary Councils and among the greater Galaxy." Elder Aaronlee smiled at the worried expression on Elder Matonae's face. "Have faith in the two sisters . . . they have proven worthy of the quest."

- Five -

The tiger joined Sasha and Adrianne as they exited Mu's gates. A damaged satellite sputtered electrical smoke outside the gates, near the jungle fringe, and the tiger growled.

"I am soon to seek oblivion," the satellite spoke as black smoke spiraled up.

"Wait," Adrianne said, halting her party.

Adrianne walked over to the satellite, and a compartment in the satellite's base opened up. A robotic hand emerged. "Take this, the memory chip of Satellite 151. Insert the chip in Satellite 263's operating panel. May Mu's previous glory be restored by you and your sister's hands." The satellite went dead.

Adrianne took the memory chip and opened the back of the satellite. In her mind, she revisited being on lockdown in the tent with Orbie. The *Popular Mechanics* magazine article, "How to rewire a Circuit," replayed in her brain. She inserted the memory chip and smoothed out the frayed circuit wires, reconnecting them to the panel. She waited, but nothing happened.

"It's fried," Sasha said. "There's nothing more you can do—"

"Just give it a minute," Adrianne urged as the tiger paced. "Alright." Adrianne sighed, and moved behind the dead satellite to recover Satellite 151's memory chip, but the back compartment was jammed shut. She screamed and kicked the satellite in frustration.

"Let's go," Adrianne said, giving up. Sasha lifted the heavy box holding the great nuclear machine as the tiger bounded ahead.

"Girl, Adrianne, I must warn, this is a most unusual course," a satellite quipped from behind.

"Orbie!" Adrianne whipped around and embraced Satellite 151.

"Satellite 151 does not comprehend," it said as it scanned the perimeter for imminent threats. "Girls, move behind Satellite 151 at once. There is large feline approaching ten paces to the right." The satellite soared ahead with fiery red laser blasters aimed.

"No, Orbie!" Adrianne screamed as the tiger charged. She leapt in between them with arms raised. "Stop!" Adrianne stroked the tiger behind the ears and it calmed.

"A most peculiar behavior from a Panthera tigris altaica," Orbie stated as it scrolled its database. "Your Tartan Clan ancestors formed powerful bonds within the animal kingdom. It appears that girl, Adrianne, also shares that gift."

"Let's keep on track," Sasha called as she walked ahead with the box. "This needs to get up and running if we are going to save them!"

"Yes." Adrianne clasped her hand onto the handle on the other side of the box to help carry the weight.

"Girl, Adrianne, and sister, Sasha, must digress to a much safer route." The satellite zipped close behind.

"Satellite 151 has coordinates. . .scrolling. . .scrolling. . . divert to—"

The two noble sisters, the tiger, and Satellite 151, scolding from behind, ventured on through the great forest of Mu in the direction of the witch's hat-shaped hill that led above, as harbingers of hope.

ᴀCKNOWLEDGEMENTS

A resounding, heartfelt, THANK YOU!! to all of my family and friends for your continued, unconditional support of my writing. Thank you, Mike (my husband and love)!

Thank you Spirit for inspiration for this story!!

Thank you to all of the Great Teachers in my life, who have guided me on this writing path (especial gratitude to bj King). ♥

Thank you, Brendan, for your beautiful artistic creations.

Also, a sincere, Thank You! to the fantastic team at Atmosphere Press for making my dream of becoming a published author a reality!

ABOUT ATMOSPHERE PRESS

Atmosphere Press is an independent, full-service publisher for excellent books in all genres and for all audiences. Learn more about what we do at atmospherepress.com.

We encourage you to check out some of Atmosphere's latest releases, which are available at Amazon.com and via order from your local bookstore:

Twisted Silver Spoons, a novel by Karen M. Wicks

Queen of Crows, a novel by S.L. Wilton

The Summer Festival is Murder, a novel by Jill M. Lyon

The Past We Step Into, stories by Richard Scharine

The Museum of an Extinct Race, a novel by Jonathan Hale Rosen

Swimming with the Angels, a novel by Colin Kersey

Island of Dead Gods, a novel by Verena Mahlow

Cloakers, a novel by Alexandra Lapointe

Twins Daze, a novel by Jerry Petersen

Embargo on Hope, a novel by Justin Doyle

Abaddon Illusion, a novel by Lindsey Bakken

Blackland: A Utopian Novel, by Richard A. Jones

The Jesus Nut, a novel by John Prather

The Embers of Tradition, a novel by Chukwudum Okeke

Saints and Martyrs: A Novel, by Aaron Roe

Author Bio

Kara Lyne Jacobson resides in the beautiful, rolling hills of Red Wing, MN with her husband and young son, Logan. She and her husband both work at the local hospital, where they first met. Born with an insatiable appetite for science fiction, Kara has always been intrigued with the notion of entire civilizations existing within the earth. She was a New Media Film Festival (2021) nominee for *The Intra-Earth Chronicles; Book I: The Two Sisters*.